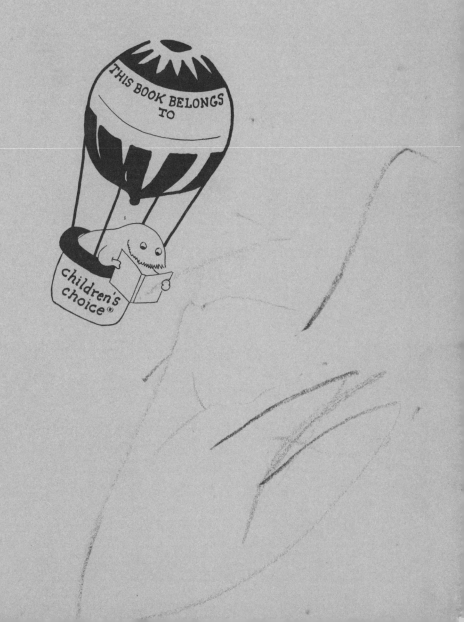

THIS BOOK BELONGS TO

children's choice®

H. A. REY

Curious George

gets a medal

Houghton Mifflin Company, Boston

A Children's Choice® Book Club Edition From Scholastic Book Services

This is George.

He lived with his friend, the man with the yellow hat.
He was a good little monkey — and always very curious.

George was alone this morning, looking at a picture
book, when the doorbell rang.

It was the mailman.

"Here is a letter for you," he said. "Put it on your friend's desk. He'll read it to you when he comes home."

George was curious. It was not often that somebody

4

wrote him. Too bad he could not read the letter — but maybe he could write one himself! In the top drawer of the desk there was paper

and ink and a fountain pen.
George sat down
on the floor
and began to write —
but the pen was dry.

It needed ink; George would have to fill it. He got a funnel from the kitchen and started pouring ink . . .

But instead of going into the pen the ink spilled all over and made a big blue puddle on the floor. It was an awful mess.

Quickly George got the blotter from the desk, but that was no help, the puddle grew bigger all the time. George had to think of something else. Why, soap and water, that's what you clean up with!

From the kitchen shelf he got a big box of soap powder and poured all the powder over the ink.

Then he pulled the garden hose through the window,

opened the tap and sprayed water on the powder.

Bubbles began to form,

and then some lather,

and more lather

and more lather

AND MORE LATHER.

In no time the whole room was full of lather,

so full, indeed, that George had to escape in a hurry . . .

When he was safely
out of the house he first
turned off the tap. But
what next? How could he
get rid of all the
lather before his
friend came home?

George sat down in the grass and
thought for a long time. Finally he had an
idea: he would get the big shovel and
shovel the lather out of the window!

But where WAS the lather? While George had been
outside thinking, it had all turned into water. Now the room
looked like a lake and the furniture like islands in it.

The shovel was no use—a pump was what George needed

to get the water out, and he knew just where to find one:
he had seen a portable pump at the farm down the road.

The farmer was away working in the fields. Nobody
noticed George when he got the pump out of the shed.

It was heavy. He would need help to pull it all the
way back to the house.

Maybe he could tie the goat
to the pump and make her pull it?
But just as George was about to slip
the loop over the goat's head —

he was hurled through the air
and landed near a pen full of pigs.

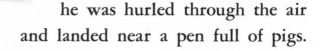

The biggest pig was standing near the gate. What if George opened the gate just enough to let him out? A big pig could easily pull a small pump.

Carefully George lifted the latch — and before he

knew it, ALL the pigs had burst out
of the pen, grunting and squealing
and trying to get away as fast as they could.
George was delighted. He had never seen anything like it.
For the moment all his troubles were forgotten . . .

But now the pigs were all gone and not a single one was
left to help him with the pump.

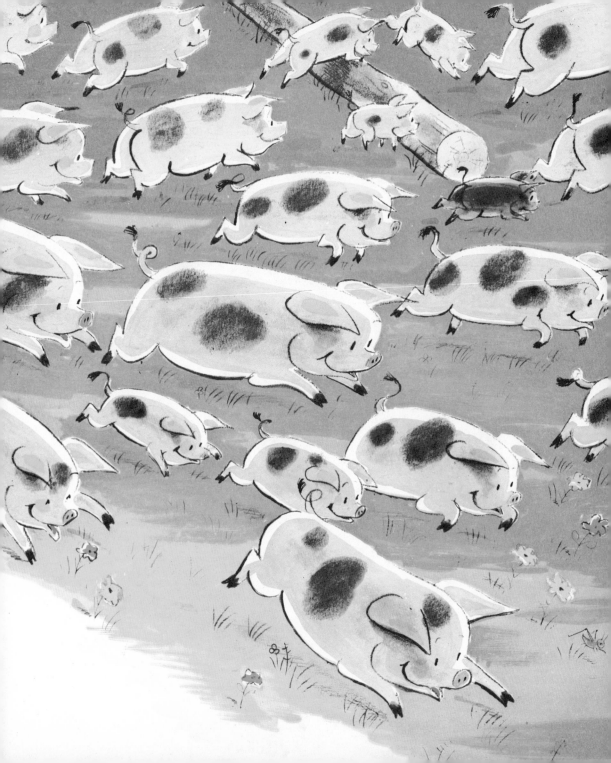

Luckily, there were cows grazing nearby. Cows were gentle and strong. It would mean nothing to a cow to pull the pump for him.

This time George was right, the cow did not mind being tied to the pump. She even let him climb on her back — and off they went! George was glad: now he would soon be home, pump out the room, and everything would be all right.

Meanwhile the farmer and his son had heard the squealing of the pigs. They rushed home from the fields and now had their hands full catching all the pigs. Not until the

24

last pig was safely back in the pen did they have time to look around. And what did they see? A little monkey riding on their cow, making off with their pump!

The chase was on.
George and the cow
were ahead at first.
But the pump was
slowing them down.
The farmers were getting
closer and closer.

Now they had almost
caught up with them — but
WHERE WAS GEORGE?

Here he was — hiding in a shirt! The farmers had run past him. But on their way home they had to come back over the same road. George did not feel safe in his hiding place . . . Just then a truck came rattling down the road.

George jumped aboard (monkeys
are good at jumping)
and was gone
before the farmers
had a chance
to see him.

The truck drove to a part of town that George had
never seen before. At last it stopped in front of a large
building. It was the Museum. George did not know what a
Museum was. He was curious. While the guard was busy
reading his paper, George slipped inside.

He walked up the steps and into a room full of all sorts of animals. At first George was scared, but then he noticed that they did not move. They were not alive, they were stuffed animals, put into the Museum so that everybody could get a good look at them.

DINOSAUR (EXTINCT)

In the next room George saw something so enormous
it took his breath away. It was a dinosaur. George was not
scared this time; he knew it was not real. He looked at the
dinosaur and then at the baby dinosaur — and then he saw

Do not touch!

BABY DINOSAUR

the palm tree full of nuts. George liked nuts. Suddenly he felt very hungry (he had missed lunch that day). He would climb up and . . . Just then he heard footsteps. He had to hide again — but where?

A family came in to take a look at the dinosaur. They paid no attention to the little monkey who was standing there. The monkey did not move. He stood so still they thought he was just another stuffed animal . . .

George was glad when they were gone! Now he could pick
the nuts. He climbed up the dinosaur's neck and started to
pull, but the nuts would not come off (George did not know
they were not real either). He pulled harder and harder,
the tree began to sway . . .

CRASH! Down came the tree on the dinosaur's head, down came the dinosaur, and down came George!

Guards came rushing in from all sides, and underneath the fallen dinosaur they found a little monkey! They pulled him out of there and brought him to Professor Wiseman who

was the director of the Museum. Professor Wiseman was
terribly angry. "Lock that naughty monkey up right away,"
he said, "and take him back to the Zoo. He must have
run away from there."

George was carried off in a cage. He felt so ashamed he almost wished he were dead . . . Suddenly the door opened. "George!" somebody shouted. It was his friend, the man with the yellow hat! "It seems you got yourself into a lot of trouble today," he said. "But maybe this letter here will get you out of it. It's from Professor Wiseman; he needs your help for an experiment. I found it on my desk at home — but I couldn't find YOU anywhere, so I came over here to talk to the Professor."

And this is what the letter said:

Dear George,

A small space ship has been built by our experimental station. It is too small for a man but could carry a little monkey. Would you be willing to go up in it?

I have never met you but I hear that you are a bright little monkey who can do all sorts of things, and that is just what we need.

We want you to do something nobody has ever done before: bail out of a space ship in flight.

When we flash you a signal you will have to open the door and bail out with the help of emergency rockets.

We hope that you are willing and that your friend will permit you to go.

Gratefully yours
Professor Wiseman
Director of the Science Museum.

DIRECTOR'S
SM
OFFICE

39

"So YOU are George!" Professor Wiseman said. "If I had only known . . . Of course everything will be forgiven, if you are willing to go."

They got the smallest size space suit for George and all the other things he needed for the flight. Then they helped him put them on and showed him how to use them. When everything was ready, a truck drove up with a special television

Check List

☑ 1 Space suit, complete with shoes & gloves

☑ 1 Space helmet

☑ 1 Oxygen tank

☑ 2 Emergency rockets

☑ 1 Parachute

screen mounted on it to watch the flight. They all got on and were off to the launching site. They checked all the controls of the space ship, especially the lever that opened the door. George tried it too.

The great moment had come. George waved goodbye and
went aboard. The door was closed. Professor Wiseman began
to count: "Five — four — three — two — one — GO!"
He pressed the button and the ship rose into the air, slowly first,

and then faster and faster and higher and higher, until
they could no longer see it in the sky. But on the screen

they saw George clearly all the time.

Now the moment had come for George to bail out.
Professor Wiseman flashed the signal. They watched the
screen: George did not move. Why didn't he pull the lever?
In a few seconds it would be too late. The ship would be
lost in outer space with George in it!

They waited anxiously . . .
At last George began to move.
Slowly, as if in a daze,
he was groping for the lever.
Would he reach it in time?
There — he had grabbed it!
The door opened —
hurrah — George
was on his way!

Out of the blue
an open parachute came floating down to earth. The truck
raced over to the spot where George would land.

What a welcome for George!

Professor Wiseman hung a big golden medal around his neck. "Because," he said, "you are the first living being to come back to earth from a space flight." And on the medal it said: To George, the First Space Monkey.

Then a newspaperman took his picture and everybody shouted and cheered, even the farmer and his son, and the kind woman from next door (who had worked for hours to get the water out of the room).

"I'm proud of you, George," said the man with the yellow
hat. "I guess the whole world is proud of you today."

It was the happiest day in George's life.

The End

The Children's Choice® Clubhouse

It's the perfect place for playing or for curling up with a good book ★ Big enough to hold a few friends (it's 3' x 4½' and 4½' tall) ★ Made of sturdy corrugated cardboard with a washable finish ★ Decorated inside and out with whimsical illustrations in full color ★ A very special gift.

To order, please send your name and address with a check or money order for $19.95 to:

**Children's Choice® Clubhouse
Scholastic Inc.
900 Sylvan Ave.
Englewood Cliffs
New Jersey 07632**